APR 1 2 2010

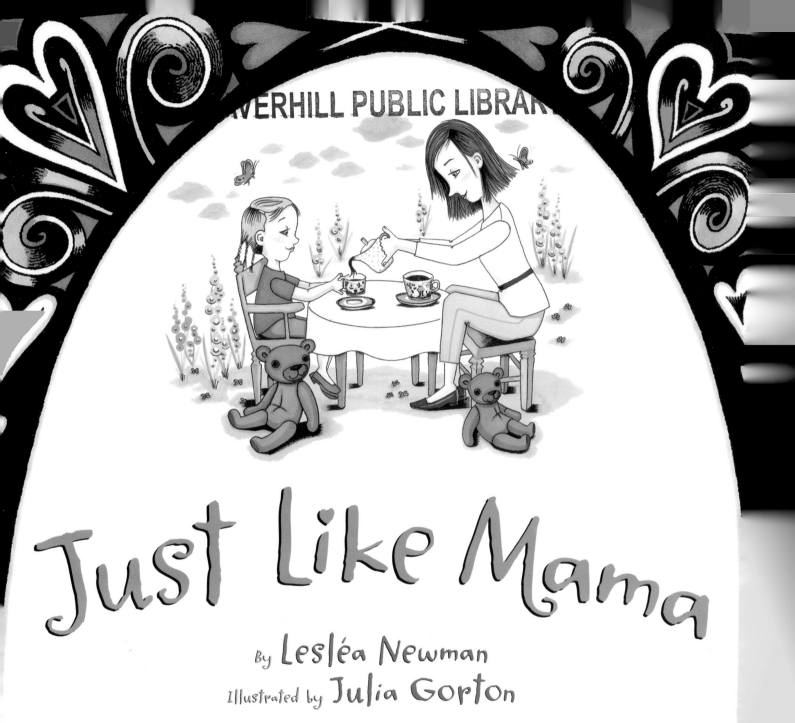

Just Like Mama

By Lesléa Newman

Illustrated by Julia Gorton

Abrams Books for Young Readers
New York

The illustrations in this book were made
with Japanese Micron pens on sketchbook paper
with Prismacolor markers.

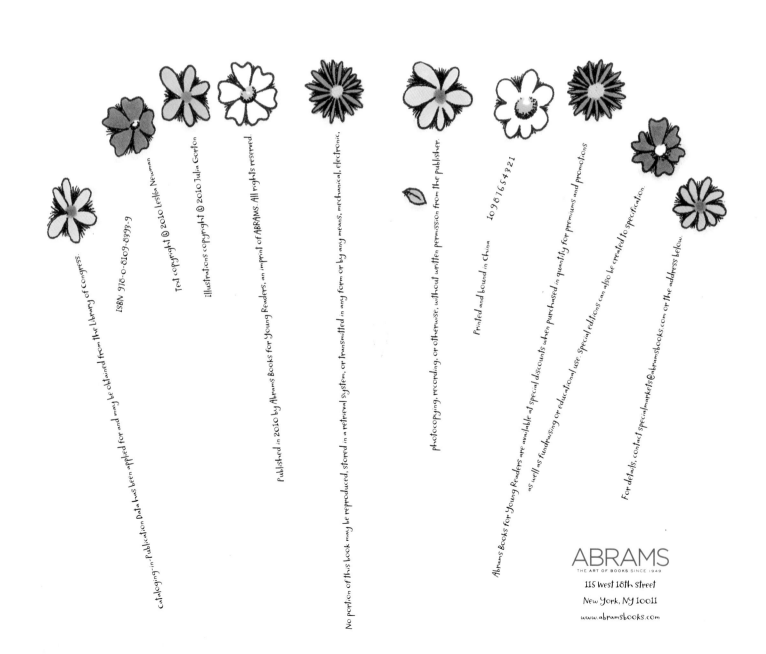

Cataloging-in-Publication Data has been applied for and may be obtained from the Library of Congress.

ISBN 978-0-8109-8393-9

Text copyright © 2010 Leslea Newman

Illustrations copyright © 2010 Julia Gorton

Published in 2010 by Abrams Books for Young Readers, an imprint of ABRAMS. All rights reserved.

No portion of this book may be reproduced, stored in a retrieval system, or transmitted in any form or by any means, mechanical, electronic, photocopying, recording, or otherwise, without written permission from the publisher.

Printed and bound in China   10 9 8 7 6 5 4 3 2 1

Abrams Books for Young Readers are available at special discounts when purchased in quantity for premiums and promotions as well as fundraising or educational use. Special editions can also be created to specification. For details, contact specialmarkets@abramsbooks.com or the address below.

ABRAMS
THE ART OF BOOKS SINCE 1949

115 West 18th Street
New York, NY 10011
www.abramsbooks.com

For my mother, with love —L. N.

. . . and for mine, too! —J. G.

With a whirl and a twirl
across the fuzzy purple rug,
she swoops down on my bed
and scoops me up into a hug.

Nobody wakes me up

just like Mama.

Half a dozen dangling braids
all hanging in a row,

then
each one tied
up tightly
with a brightly
colored bow.

Nobody
combs my hair
just like
Mama.

A pile of apple
pancakes,
each one shaped
into a moon,

and cocoa with a cloud of cream, stirred with her special spoon.

Nobody cooks breakfast just like Mama.

In her funny flowered hat
and her sunny yellow clogs,

she pulls up weeds,
and waters seeds,

and helps me
hunt for frogs.

Nobody gardens
just like Mama.

She sets out cups and saucers
for my teddy bears
and me,
then shows us all
the proper way
to pour a pot
of tea.

Nobody
has
tea parties
just like Mama

and a
swirly straw
to sip
my milk
served on a
silver tray.

Nobody
makes lunch
just like Mama.

In a cozy, comfy chair, on her cozy, comfy lap,

She clasps her hands together
and her arms become a loop,
so I can bounce my ball three times
and throw it through the hoop.

Nobody plays ball

just like Mama.

In a graceful gown that glitters like a starry sky at night,

She's a lion tamer teaching me to roar with all my might.

Nobody plays
dress-up
just like
Mama.

A mountain of spaghetti that we gobble and we slurp, and when we can't eat one more bite, we both sit back and burp.

In a corner by the window,
in our favorite rocking chair,
she softly sings a lullaby
while brushing out my hair.

Nobody rocks me just like Mama.

With kisses on
my forehead
and my eyelids
left and right,

she whispers,
"Sweet dreams,
Sweetie Pie,"

and then turns out the light.

Nobody

loves me
just like Mama.